KING

OF

MERCY

CLAIRE ELIZABETH GROSE

DEDICATION

This book is dedicated to
Ashleigh and Trent
My beloved Granddaughter and Partner

CONTENTS

PREFACE

Two things I just wanted to say about this book are, why I started writing and how I came by the title.

I grew up in the 1950's-1960's in Adelaide, South Australia, my life was pretty simple but wonderful. I was very lucky to have a secure family life, and my Mum and Dad brought the family up to treat others with respect, do the right thing, be courteous, and respect your elders. We had a strict upbringing and even as adults our parents never criticized us but encouraged us to do our best in life. They were "Aussie battlers" but we always managed to make it through the tough times!

They were people of integrity and cared about others and instilled that into our family.

Church was a big part of our lives growing up. We went to Sunday School at an early age and progressed up through the appropriate groups as we got older.

Youth groups, camps and church anniversaries were all important to the whole family. We competed in church sports teams, basketball and tennis with other parishes across Adelaide. Life-long friendships were in the making and cherished golden memories to look back on that would never fade.

Bible stories, hymns and choruses were all part of getting to know Jesus. This nurturing finally led me to the day Jesus came knocking on my heart's door. Being filled with the Holy Spirit is something I will never forget and the overwhelming power of His love that filled my whole being and propelled me to the front of the hall to give my heart to Him. No words can fully describe the joy I felt. That was in February 1968, I was 14 years of age. He has been my Shining Light ever since, and lives within me always.

So I thank my beautiful Mum and Dad for the way they raised me and for the foundation of knowing Jesus' love.

It was in His love that I started to write, in the autumn of 1993. My journey has brought me to this book "King of Mercy", because in His Word, His mercy is renewed every morning. "The Lord's unfailing love and mercy still continue, fresh as the morning, as sure as the sunrise." Lamentations 3:22-23. Good News Bible.

He is the King of Mercy in every way because He took our sin to The Cross, and replaced it with His forgiveness, which has given us eternal life, to all who believe that He died on the Cross at Calvary and three days later rose to life by His Heavenly Father who gave us the Holy Spirit. The Lord is now seated at the right hand of God in His heavenly Kingdom.

What a revelation to rely on, knowing He is always ready to supply all our needs, we only have to ask and believe that we will receive.

When I was a young Christian reading my Bible was really important to me in getting to know Jesus as my personal Saviour and became the foundation that I built my faith on.

It gave me strength and courage as I began life in the workforce at the age of 16. Coming from a sheltered upbringing it was my life-line to self-confidence and adapting to social life at work.
The poems reflect the everyday feelings and emotions that we feel as we meet the challenges of life and how the great magnitude of God's love can help us rise above them.

Many of these writings have been my first words of whispered prayer, so much that I have been moved to write them down at once and continue on in His wonderful and absolute love.

Together we write as He provides my inspiration.

All glory to Him, my precious Lord Jesus!

ACKNOWLEDGEMENTS

My heartfelt thanks to my beloved family, my Mum and Dad, Lilly and Ken, and my siblings Jeanette, June, Carol, Gloria and Lynne, for their never ending encouragement and support to me. To the rest of the family, you are all a precious link that joins us together.

To Michael and Andrew for your continual support to me in fulfilling my passion of writing poems for the Lord to help others through His Word.

A huge thank you to Junie for editing my poems and the coffees and lunches we enjoyed along the way.

To Joy Furnell for her Crown of Thorns drawing, you have an amazing gift, thank you Joy.

A special thank you to Salisbury Uniting Church, Adelaide for photos, used by permission.

A big thank you to Carol, Dennis, Lynne, Michael and Andrea, for great photos.

To my friends and Church Families, thank you for your love and support.

To my beautiful sons, Michael and Andrew, and your families. Thank you for loving me, and I am so glad He gave you to me. I cherish my grandchildren, Ashleigh, Costa, Lailah and Jaxon. I love you all so much.

To you the reader, thank you for picking this book up and I pray you will find His peace and love on the pages ahead.

May He shower you all with His love and blessings.

PART ONE

"Lord, I know you will never stop being merciful to me. Your love and loyalty will always keep me safe."

Psalm 40 : 11

THANK YOU LORD…
YOUR FAITHFULNESS NEVER ENDS…

"The Lord's unfailing love and mercy still
continue, fresh as the morning, as sure as the sunrise."

Lamentations 3 : 22 - 23

MY DAILY PRAYER

Be with me, stay with me,
Close by my side,
Fill me with your peace and love,
So my spirit shall surely fly
To the heights in your love,
As only you can give,
Prepare me for this day ahead,
So in me you'll always live.

YOUR GRACE AND MERCY

Lord Your grace and mercy
Such a beautiful thing,
Available to all who believe in You
And claim You "King of Kings".

Such a precious gift
To all mankind,
Your grace and mercy endures
A pardon for all time.

Your loving heart so full,
Enough for all the world,
We only need to seek You,
Why You love us You will tell.

Your grace and mercy Lord
Can be ours today
A gift from You alone Lord
To each heart is on its way!

STREAMS OF SWEET FRAGRANCE

Streams of sweet fragrance
Carry the love of God,
Straight to the heart
Which accepts His words of love.

Our praise and worship whispers
Are heard in the Heavens above
Through streams of sweet fragrance,
Carrying the love of God.

So delicate and pure
Notes descend to the soul,
Offering balm to anoint
Making your spirit whole.

Streams of sweet fragrance
A never ending flow,
Bringing our praises to God
Where He sits on His glorious Throne.

HEAVEN'S STORE

Heaven's store is always open,
Its doors are never closed,
You are served a lifetime
From the Saviour's glorious Throne.

He has everything you need
And it comes with grace divine,
His Holy Spirit will guide you
If you lose your way sometimes.

There's plenty of choice to suit every need,
Whether it be healing, comfort or strength,
The Saviour's supply is boundless,
To His store there is no end.

Heaven's store has wealth in mercy
Given by His pierced hands
That you will take ever so gently
From the mark that revealed God's plan.

Yes Heaven's store is always open
Every hour, day or night,
You can never take too much,
He's already paid for your supplies.

ONLY THE SAVIOUR

Only the Saviour can hold
The stars in His hands,
As recorded in His Word
The universe was His plan.

Our lives are so complex,
Creation a miracle indeed,
Only the Saviour could make
Everything we see.

The bowels of the earth
Give forth wealth untold,
The treasure in the flora
Gives us joy to behold.

Only the Saviour could reveal
The loved ones we have,
He puts us together
To fulfil His Holy plan.

Each one of us a seed
Sown by His hand,
Only the Saviour could create
The miracle of man!

SPRINGTIME HARVEST

Morning song so sweet,
The Master hears them all,
Peace reigns supreme,
Early morning wake up call.

His birds nourish gardens
For the harvest to come,
Springtime at its best,
Gardens beauty from the Son.

Everything has a reason
According to His plan,
The harvest will come
By His appointed command.

Yes Mother Nature's jewel
When she feels the call,
Is God's crowning beauty
Springtime harvest; gifts for all.

GOD'S LOVE IS A JOURNEY

Our love for the Almighty
Is a journey indeed,
Taking decades to evolve
Will bring us to our knees.

To accept the Holy Spirit's call
Is where it begins,
To see His golden light
And feel His love within.

A washing of your spirit
Will surely take place,
Your heart will feel changes
As you live in His grace.

This journey will deepen
As challenges come to life,
Shadows will come and go
As you walk in His light.

Jesus will equip you
For the journey of life,
As you travel
In a love you cannot hide!

HIS LOVE FOR ALL

His love for all people of the world
Bears no bars,
His love for all is paramount
He will love you from the stars.

He craves your attention
No matter who you are,
He made you in His image,
He loves you from afar.

He gave us the world to live in
With wealth to reap,
Precious gems below the earth
Abundant gifts to seek.

The Lord's love never fails
And He craves to be called
Into the hearts of all mankind,
The King of Mercy loves us all.

YOUR BEAUTY LORD…
IS ALL AROUND US…

"He is good to everyone and has
compassion on all he made."

Psalm 145 : 9

RICHES OF THE EARTH

The riches of the earth Lord
That You made for us,
Lay above and beneath,
You gave us through Your love.

Precious Lord Your gifts
Of gems that sparkle and shine,
And a wealth of infrastructure
Is what we will find.

You gave us trees and plants
To delight our very soul,
The rivers, valleys and fields
Serve our purposes untold.

Healing oils and balms
That come from centuries of time,
Frankincense, Myrrh and Gold
Were Your gifts from the Magi.

Yes all the riches of earth
That Your mighty hands have made,
Your wealth beyond our understanding;
I pray mankind will give thanks some day.

GARDENS LUSH

Gardens lush,
There's gladness in the air,
Time to wake His beauty
From plants and flowers everywhere.

The birds are singing,
His beauty so profound,
Everything fresh and new
Makes me stop to look around.

Colour by His hand,
None other can suffice,
Brings wonder and awe
Gardens lush for my delight!

The simple things of life,
New born lambs; buds burst forth,
No matter who you are
Will bring such joy.

Now it's time for sunshine rays
To melt the snow and ice,
Gardens lush with aromas sweet,
His beauty comes alive!

HOLY SPIRIT'S LOVE

Holy Spirit's love so real
It can't be ignored,
So if you try,
He will love you even more!

The Holy Spirit's love
Will wash away your sin,
Inside your heart
He will make His home within.

He will fill you with rapture
As He brings heaven near,
Sent by the Father
To comfort and take your fears.

Holy Spirit's love so special,
No words can explain,
Such pure joy He brings,
Precious, He will remain!

FOOD FOR MY SOUL

Food for my soul is
Found in His Word
And in this world around me,
So much to learn.

Food for my soul is
The gentle lapping tide
And the sun glistening on water,
That's joy I just can't hide.

Food for my soul is
Springtime flowers,
The wealth of God's beauty,
Hour after hour.

Food for my soul is
A forest of eucalyptus and pine
After the rain its scent
Thrills this heart of mine.

Food for my soul is
His rainbow in the sky,
God's creation of the world
Only by Him, so divine!

Yes Lord, food for my soul
Is all around,
Because of You
True love I have found.

EARLY MORNING GLORIES

I see early morning glories
When I'm alone with You
That's surely what I find Lord
As sun shines on morning dew.

Your beauty I see
In blossoms sweet,
Wild flowers line the highway
Early morning glories I meet

A spotlight through the clouds
A beam from sky to sea,
Brings a thrill to my soul
Can only be from Thee.

An overcast sky
Cannot shadow my soul,
Early morning glories
Come one hundred fold.

Yes, early morning glories Lord
Take my heart away,
Delights everywhere
They will never fade.

DRINK YOU IN LORD

I want to drink You in Lord
Every day of my life,
A never ending presence
That is my guiding light.

A light that is golden
And sparkles so divine,
Its beams reaching out
To touch this heart of mine.

It's then I want to drink You in,
Your Spirit shining bright,
The ever presence within me
That lifts me to the heights.

I want to drink You in Lord,
Your aroma sweet and pure,
So I will never thirst again,
In You my life secure!

CELEBRATE

Celebrate God's love,
The love He has for you,
Nothing else compares
To refresh and renew.

Celebrate God's love
That lives forever in your heart,
All believers will receive a reward
When they follow His holy path.

Celebrate God's love
In a union personal and true,
The love of God so complete
Through His Spirit He sends to you.

Celebrate God's love
Every day of your life,
His grace and mercy surround you
So you can walk in His glorious light.

YOUR WORDS

Thank You Lord for Your words
That thrill my soul,
They bring me out of the dark
To make me whole.

They fill me with awe
In Your mercy so deep,
They give me special joy
That is complete.

Your words are forever,
They will never fade,
As sure as the sunrise
Calling the day!

Your words are our lifeline
Of that I'm sure,
They bring comfort and healing,
That's what Your grace is for.

Yes Father, Your love is Divine,
Nothing can compare,
You are the King of Mercy
We need you everywhere!

HERE WITH ME

I'm so glad Lord
You are here with me,
Through Your Holy Spirit,
Your love I receive.

So sweetly He brings,
Tides of Your love
That sweep over me
To build me up.

Throughout my life
He has brought You close,
Those moments of rapture
Bring me joy and hope.

My heart rejoices
That I'm not alone
Because You are here with me
My life You own.

BEAUTIFUL DUSK

I'm always in awe when dusk arrives,
She looks her best,
Puffy clouds change colour
When the sun bows down for rest.

I can't help but stop
To watch her changing views,
My favourite colours displayed
In musky pinks and blues.

I feel Your presence Lord
In the beautiful dusk You send,
Heavenly rays displayed
Beyond horizon's end.

So thank You Lord for beautiful dusk,
Designed by Your hand,
A presence so comforting,
She is ruled by Your command.

CONNECT WITH HIM…
EVERY DAY IN PRAYER…

"Let us be brave, then, and approach God's throne,
where there is grace. There we will receive mercy
and find grace to help us just when we need it."

Hebrews 4 : 16

I COME TO YOU LORD

I come to You Lord in praise
To acknowledge Your love for me,
I come before You as Your child
Because You set me free.

I come to You Lord so humbly,
I know I walk in Your light,
My past hasn't been easy
But You will help me to survive.

I come to You Lord in trust
With no shadow of a doubt,
My future is in Your hands,
I believe it is all laid out.

I come to You Lord in the love
That You gave to me,
You are my rock and my refuge,
I bow down and worship Thee.

BECAUSE YOU ARE LOVE LORD

Because You are love Lord,
We are saved;
When we believe in You
Your Spirit comes to stay.

Because You are love Lord,
To You there is no end,
We can approach You
Through Your Spirit that You send.

Because You are love Lord,
We have the promise of new life,
Our sins are forgiven
In You, the risen Christ.

Because You are love Lord,
We can live again,
Your promise to every believing heart
That will take You in.

Yes we can walk in Your light
Every day of our lives,
Because You are love Lord;
Our glorious risen Christ.

GOD'S KNOWLEDGE AND WISDOM

God's knowledge and wisdom can be yours
When an honest request is made,
He will guide your right decision
Because from your heart it came.

His power and glory will shine on you
Because you acted in your faith,
There is no other way,
From His supply you can take.

You can be sure His plan will open
When you call on His wisdom today,
As you concede to His will
That is the only way.

Yes His knowledge and wisdom are yours,
When you claim it in His name,
He loves you beyond words,
You will be amazed!

THE FAMILY HE GAVE TO ME

Sometimes life seems empty
As we look back over the years,
In our prime life was hectic
Where did they go those years?

Memories flood back from yesterday
As clear as can be,
My childhood and teenage years
Were so wonderful for me.

The Lord was part of our family,
We said "Grace" before every meal,
An anchor in our lives,
Peace and assurance was so real.

A simple but wonderful life
We had growing up,
Battlers through the years
But we always had enough.

Love and respect were utmost
As we shared each other's hurts,
Which we made "a matter of prayer"
Left in God's hands where they were nursed!

So I look back with much love
On the family He gave to me,
I couldn't have been happier,
In His care we always will be.

PART TWO

"To him who is able to keep you from falling and
to bring you faultless and joyful before his
glorious presence – to the only God our
Saviour, through Jesus Christ our Lord, be glory,
majesty, might, and authority, from all ages past, and
now, and forever and ever! Amen."

Jude 1 : 24

TELL HIM YOUR EVERYTHING…
AND RECEIVE HIS TENDER CARE…

"And yet, because your mercy is great….
You are a gracious and merciful God!"

Nehemiah 9 : 31

SPEND TIME WITH GOD

Spend time with God
Whenever you can,
Make it a priority
Because He is the great "I Am".

Spend time with God,
You're a disciple worthwhile,
Receive His calm and peace
And think of Him for awhile.

He adores you so much,
He took the Cross for you,
He paid for your eternal life
So you could be renewed.

Spend time with God,
Quietly read His Word,
You will feel a connection,
You He came to serve!

YOU ARE MY SHIELD

You are my shield and comfort
Wherever I go,
I can talk to You anytime,
That I truly know.

I can carry You anywhere,
Day or night You are here,
You never leave me,
My faith keeps You near.

I can rely on Your mercy and grace,
It's only my cares that weigh me down,
When I learn to give them to You,
I'll wear a smile not a frown.

Yes, You are my shield and comfort Lord,
My prayers I claim in Your Name,
You are the Lord Almighty,
You will never change!

STRONG IN YOUR LOVE

Help me stay strong in Your love Lord
When life plays tricks on me,
Help me overcome
The hurdles that I see.

Help me to be strong Lord
In You my guide and strength,
Through the trials I face Lord
Be my one defence.

Help me to stay strong Lord
Against the demands of life,
To carry an honest heart
That is generous and kind.

Keep me strong in Your love Lord
As only You can do,
Because of Your precious Holy Spirit,
I truly love You.

I NEED YOU LORD

Every second, every hour
I need You Lord,
To get me through today
So I can rise above the storm.

I need Your shining light
To brighten my steps,
To highlight my path
So I can see ahead.

I need Your precious hand
To take hold of mine,
The strength in Your grasp
Can only be from "The Divine".

Yes, I need You Lord,
That no words can explain,
Your never ending supply of love
Comes to me each day!

YOU LIFT ME UP

Lord, I love the way You lift me up
When in trust I come to You,
I believe You hear my prayers
That's all I have to do.

It's peace and calm I know,
Earthly cares just slip away,
I'm lost in Your sweet love
That I can call on any day.

You lift me up to heal me,
My energy restored,
My faith and trust so real,
It's You I adore.

So, thank You Lord for helping me,
Your comfort so divine,
I love the way You lift me up,
I'm so glad You are mine.

RENEW MY HEART

Renew my heart Lord,
To a happy state,
Where Your Spirit can flow
In Your mercy and grace.

Renew my heart Lord
With Your light that shines,
A powerful healing beam
Into this soul of mine.

Renew my heart Lord,
Though shadows I still see,
Help me to rise above them
To safety in Thee.

Lord I need You now
And Your Spirit Divine,
Come close to me this moment,
Renew this heart of mine.

CONFIDE IN THE SAVIOUR…
HE'S ALWAYS BY YOUR SIDE…

"And yet the Lord is waiting to be merciful to you. He
is ready to take pity on you because he always does what is right.
Happy are those who put their trust in the Lord."

Isaiah 30 : 18

YOUR FAITHFULNESS IS FOREVER

Your faithfulness is forever Lord,
When I'm busy You still want me,
Sometimes I'm focused on my chores
I forget to talk to Thee.

Your faithfulness astounds me;
Am I worthy of Your smile?
You wait so patiently
For me to talk to You a while.

Your faithfulness never leaves me,
When I sleep You watch over me,
Your golden light casts a beam
So I'm in Your care constantly.

Yes Lord, Your faithfulness never tires,
It's as sure as the rising dawn,
I fall to my knees to thank You,
You make me love You more and more.

LIGHT OF LOVE

His light of love will shine
Like a thousand stars,
Even brighter than the sun,
To love you from afar.

His light of love; a beam
That will never dim,
To make you a bright star
To shine for Him.

His light of love will soothe
The strongest pain you know,
On a broken heart or worried mind
His healing oil will flow.

Invite His light of love,
You will never lose but win,
His Paradise is yours,
Believe; He will take you in.

POWER ME

Power me through today Lord
With Your energy and strength,
Give me purpose for today
From Your supply that I need.

Power me through today Lord,
Give me a mountain top view,
So I can rise above my challenges
To clear skies in You.

Power me through today Lord,
May the hours come to pass
With Your tender loving care,
For everything I ask.

Power me through today Lord
With Your hand on my back,
Keep me looking forward
So nothing will I lack.

OPEN YOUR HEART

Open your heart to the Saviour,
He's the lover of your soul,
Confess to Him your heart desires
So His plan for you will unfold.

Your trust and faith are the tools
That He needs to do His work,
So His desires will be yours
Like tender buds they'll be nursed.

Open your heart to the Saviour
So He can tend to your needs,
He will bind up your wounds
And care for them tenderly.

Give Him your cares today
From your heart that yearns His touch,
Be assured He will deal with them
Because He loves you so very much.

PASS HIS MESSAGE ON

Pass His message on
When it's laid upon your heart,
The Holy Spirit will prompt you
To the place where you can start.

He will give you confidence
To pass His message on,
That small voice inside you
Is heard in the realms beyond!

Pass His message on
To give hope to the lost,
Forgiveness is waiting
When they come to Jesus' Cross!

His Mercy and Grace reigns
With the promise of freedom for life,
So pass His message on
So the darkness is turned to light.

I'M NOT ALONE

I'm not alone Lord,
The Spirit is always with me,
I feel Him close
And know He comforts me.

He brings the realms of Heaven
To believing hearts,
The love of God
He can impart.

I'm not alone
Though some days I feel low,
It's then I can rest
In His love that I know.

I can reach for Your Word Lord,
A sure comfort to me,
I'm not alone
Because The Spirit lives in me.

I'm not alone
No matter how I feel,
The Holy Spirit lives within
I'm covered by His Seal.

TURN TO HIM…
SO HE CAN HEAL YOU…

"May God our Father and the Lord Jesus
Christ give you grace and peace."

Ephesians 1 : 2

THE FLOODGATES WILL OPEN

When you accept the Saviour,
The floodgates will open within,
He sends His Holy Spirit to you,
You are forgiven of your sin.

The floodgates will open,
Compassion and kindness flow through,
Together with the Spirit's pure love
You are renewed.

Your cares and doubts are the stones
That hurt your tender feet,
But you need not worry
He is all you need.

Yes, the floodgates will open,
His divine love will own your soul,
Your heart is now swept clean
For you are now made whole.

The floodgates wide open,
He will wash your wounds away,
The floodgates wide open,
In His care you will remain.

HE IS LOVE HE IS LIGHT

He is love, He is light,
He calls for peace and calm
To live a righteous life,
To love each other was His command.

To care for our fellow man
And have love in our heart,
To use compassion and kindness
Is where we can start.

He is love, He is light,
His Word tells us so,
Because we are His beloved
His love to us will flow.

He is love, He is light,
What more can we need,
He is our Saviour
We are His children indeed!

GOLDEN TEARDROPS

Golden teardrops from Heaven,
You will surely know
When they appear in your heart,
God's presence they will show.

These golden moments with God
Will make your heart shine,
Golden teardrops from Heaven
Will mend this soul of mine.

The Holy Spirit's presence,
So dear, so divine
Will send those golden teardrops
Just at the right time.

Golden teardrops will flow,
A balm to heal
Any hurts and scars
That life has revealed.

Golden teardrops are a sign
That God's forgiveness is yours,
He will send them from His Throne
As His angels applaud!

CARRY A GRATEFUL HEART

Carry a grateful heart
For what the Saviour has done for you,
Your faith is all He needs
To help you through and through.

Carry a grateful heart
For the strength He has supplied
On those weary days
When on Him you had to rely.

Carry a grateful heart
When He celebrates with you,
Joy beyond compare
From the reward He gave to you.

Carry a grateful heart
For the humble things of life,
Give thanks for what you have
And that you walk in His light.

Be so grateful to the Saviour
For the friends He placed on your path,
Who brought joy to your journey
And a sweet fragrance to your heart!

GOD'S PEACE

God's peace is around you
When you rely on His love,
From the realms of Heaven
He lifts you up.

Ask for His calm and peace
To serve you through the day,
Claim it on His Blood of Calvary
It is the only way.

Your trust and faith will rise
As you receive your request,
So faithful is His love
For you to do your best.

God's peace will surround you
With tender loving care,
We are His children,
He will linger with you there.

GOD'S SHINING LIGHT

Your shining light Lord
Is a beacon to me,
Filled with endless power
Searching over humanity.

You are the God Almighty
Heaven's Holy Son,
You are love itself,
Brighter than the sun.

Your shining light will beckon
And bring wonder to behold,
Your power and Your glory
For every heart and soul.

Your golden lights are rapture
From Heaven's Holy realm,
A divine endowment
That will surely overwhelm.

Your shining light brings awe
In great magnitude,
A blessing so divine
That joins me to You.

THE LAMB OF GOD…
IS THE KING OF MERCY…

"…I will forgive their sins and I will no longer remember their wrongs. I, the Lord, have spoken."

Jeremiah 31 : 34

GOD LOOKS INTO YOUR HEART

God looks into each heart,
He sees our joys and doubts,
As lovers of His Word,
Good seeds we must give out.

He loves a righteous heart
That tries to do its best,
There's no place for selfishness,
A good heart will stand the test.

God looks into the heart,
He yearns for love and truth,
To obey His commands
Is what we need to do.

So thank You Holy Father
For calling us Your own,
Help us to live the life You want
So our final rest will be Your home!

ENCOURAGEMENT FOR THE SOUL

We all need food for the soul
To nourish our love for God,
For reassurance and peace
That we fall short on.

Encouragement for the soul
Comes in many ways,
Opening and reading His Word
Or through music His love is displayed.

Your trust will mature
As you journey in your faith,
His beloved are there to help you
Every step of the way.

Claim His love for strength,
The Holy Spirit will supply,
Encouragement for your soul;
On Him you can rely!

GOD'S ETERNAL FLAME

God's eternal flame,
A torch for all mankind
Is His light of love
Pure joy is what you'll find.

It will shine forever,
A beacon for every path
In everyone's life,
For His guidance; just ask.

God's eternal flame,
A source of healing and peace,
Call for the Saviour today,
Your needs He will meet.

God's eternal flame
Will burn within your heart,
A golden light forever
On you has left its mark.

ETERNAL GIVER OF LIFE

Our precious Lord Jesus,
Eternal giver of life,
You will come with Your rewards
To make everything right.

Eternal giver of life;
When we offer our heart to You,
You will care for us tenderly
As You help us through and through.

Eternal giver of life;
Our home You will provide,
We can spend forever
Close by Your side.

You are the great Redeemer,
Almighty God in glory and power,
We can call You into our life,
This moment, this very hour!

ETERNAL LOVE

You are eternal love Lord,
Maker of all we see,
But The Spirit is Your greatest gift,
You bring us to our knees.

You are eternal love
When it comes to the heart,
We can receive the Holy Spirit,
That's where we can start.

Eternal love comes with mercy and grace
That only God can give,
But through His Holy Spirit,
These gifts can you receive.

You are eternal love,
Who paid the price of Calvary,
You loved us all so much,
Through You we can be free.

CRUX OF THE MATTER

The crux of the matter Lord
Is to live the Christian life,
By accepting You into the heart
So we can see The Spirit's light.

You came to the world
To show us how to live,
To have a heart of kindness
With compassion and care to give.

To lend a hand to our fellow man
Is paramount to You Lord,
To show them Your love
So Heaven's angels will applaud.

The crux of the matter Lord
Is to receive You; The Son of Man,
And to declare You are the Saviour
Who fulfilled God's Holy plan!

THE WRANGLES OF MY HEART

Lord, lift me above
The wrangles of my heart,
Give me the strength
To jump the shadows on my path.

I can feel relief
When I lift my gaze
To Your heavenly help
That You send every day.

I can surrender it all
And confess the truth,
In trust and faith I believe
You're here to help me through.

The wrangles of my heart
I should leave alone,
In Your appointed time
I will be shown.

COMING OUT OF WINTER

Coming out of winter,
His glory shines so bright,
Deep within my soul
Because He is my shining light.

Coming out of winter
I've left those hurts behind,
I'm walking in His light,
The glorious Christ Divine.

I'm coming out of winter,
My cup overflows
With His grace and mercy,
Because Jesus I know.

I'm coming out of winter,
My future looking bright,
Shining like the stars
Because it feels so right.

Yes, I'm coming out of winter,
I hold His pierced hand,
My heart refreshed and renewed,
Now it's time to see His plan.

BRAND NEW

The Holy Spirit so patient
Waits for your call
To invite Him into your heart
To be your all.

He brings comfort and love
Beyond words untold,
With God's anointing balm
You are made whole.

As sinners we come
To be washed clean,
It's then His Spirit's showers
In your life will be seen.

His golden light will shine,
Now you are made brand new
Within your heart forever,
No matter what you do.

He will never leave you,
He's heaven's healer and guide,
You will be brand new
Because He's always by your side.

GOD'S STREAM OF SUPPLY

God's stream of supply,
An endless store of strength,
To call on everyday
For everything you need.

This stream never runs dry,
It's ripples gentle and clear,
Glorious colours within
To thrill each heart so dear.

God's stream of supply is for all
To bathe and be healed,
From the scars and wounds of life
That to us are so real.

God's stream flows with fragrance
So pure and so sweet,
To thrill the heart and soul
That makes us feel complete.

Yes, God's stream of supply
Beckons hearts to come,
To bathe in His balm
Of never ending love.

ARMS OF TRUST

Lay in the arms of trust,
The Saviour will soothe your weary heart,
When the weight is too heavy
He'll share the load on your path.

Lay in the arms of the Saviour,
No purer love you will find,
His glory will shine around you
And lift you up every time.

Lay in the arms of trust
They will never let you down,
Cast your cares on the Saviour,
No surer help is found.

Lay in the arms of trust
For peace and calm within,
Claim His help every day,
He wants you to come to Him.

GRACE AND MERCY EVERY DAY

I need Your grace and mercy Lord,
Every day of my life,
I need Your guidance Lord
To make my day so right.

I need Your grace and mercy
To keep my thoughts in check,
There's no place for guilt or shame,
Or reflecting on regret.

What's done is done,
It can't be changed,
But living in Your grace and mercy
I can face today.

So, I need Your grace and mercy Lord,
To sustain my faith and trust,
You took Your Cross to Calvary
Follow You I must.

PART THREE

"Happy are those who are merciful to others;
God will be merciful to them!"

Matthew 5 : 7

RECEIVE HIS BLESSINGS…
EVERY DAY…

"May mercy, peace, and love be yours in full measure."

Jude 1 : 2

DIVINE INTERVENTION

The Holy Spirit comes silently
To touch the soul,
Divine intervention
Will make you whole.

He brings God's pure love
To live in your heart,
He dwells within
For you to make a new start.

He will change you from the inside
Through your thoughts and cares,
The heavenlies you'll know
Because He lingers there.

You will live more in your faith
That will shine like the stars,
Your love in Him secure
Because that's who you are.

Yes, divine intervention will make you shine
To reflect the love of God,
A flame within you,
A presence you lean upon.

SEAL OF LOVE

Holy Spirit's seal of love
So deep and real,
Endless His supply
Comes with Heaven's Holy seal.

Quietly He comes
He brings the Saviour's love,
From Heaven's precious realm,
To all who invite Him; "come".

A feeling of warmth
And surrender so real,
The Holy Spirit's love
You will truly feel.

His anointing and presence
Will heal the deepest wound,
He will pour God's Holy Oil
To heal precious you!

The Holy Spirit's seal of love
Will never come undone,
You are saved for ever
With God's own precious Son.

STREAMS OF GRACE AND MERCY

Streams of grace and mercy Lord
Flow from Your Throne,
To every soul on earth
Who You call Your own.

Streams of grace and mercy,
A pardon for our sin,
Though shame we may feel,
From the Cross You took us in.

God's gift of grace and mercy,
Through Jesus Christ our Lord,
We no longer have to carry guilt,
You paid once and for all.

In streams of grace and mercy,
Living waters sparkle and shine,
No more condemnation,
You give the gift of Eternal Life.

SOARING WITH GOD

To soar with God
In the heavens above,
Faith and trust is required
When to Him you succumb.

Soaring with God
Is when relief floods your heart,
You feel free inside,
Your healing can start.

Soaring with God,
Your cup will overflow,
Indescribable joy
You will surely know.

Your victories will be many
As you abide in His light,
Take hold of His redemption,
To fulfil your life.

YOUR GREATNESS

Many see Your greatness Lord
And have Your love within,
Your power and glory so evident
A new life will begin.

Man cannot understand
The magnitude of Your love,
Your greatness so overwhelming
From You the Precious Son.

Your supply to us is boundless
From Your Holy realm,
Privilege powers are only
For those who have left this world.

So thank You Lord for Your greatness
Beyond the human mind,
The best is yet to come
To Your beloved in our mankind.

A glorious beginning is waiting
In Your Kingdom above,
Your greatness will be revealed
When that glorious day comes.

REASONS

The Lord has His reasons
And a plan for each of us
Devised in the beginning
Like the dawn and the dusk.

Only He knows
The how and the why,
We are not to question
But to accept His will on high.

The Lord has His reasons
And lessons for us to learn,
He loves us so dearly,
Over us He surely yearns.

He gave us the power of choice
To make decisions in our lives,
We have to learn by our mistakes
And by His grace we can survive.

His reasons are complex
And one day we will know,
When we come face to face
With the Saviour on His Throne.

OPEN YOUR HEART TO RECEIVE…
HIS ETERNAL MERCY…

"The Lord will take delight in you, and
in his love he will give you new life."

Zephaniah 3 : 17

MANIFEST GOD'S LOVE

Manifest God's love,
A love for all time,
The heart of the heavenlys
He gave to mankind.

Manifest God's love,
A love that knows no end,
Brought by His Holy Spirit,
His love to us He sends.

Manifest God's love
That shines for all the world,
A beacon for His glory
That His ministry unfurled.

Manifest God's love,
Your gift of Eternity,
Claim Him your King of Kings
You will live eternally.

PROFOUND PEACE

When touched by the Holy Spirit
Profound peace fills my heart,
Nothing else seems to matter
Those moments leave their mark.

A baptism of pure love
Will dim your deepest care,
When touched by the Holy Spirit
Is joy beyond compare.

Profound peace known to me
When the Holy Spirit acts,
My heart and soul respond
Nothing do I lack!

He comforts, heals and guides me,
Enough thanks I can't reveal,
Profound peace fills my soul,
A love that is so real!

QUIET WHISPERS

Jesus hears your quiet whispers
And cares for each one,
Wrapped tenderly in His sure love
His answers will come.

He treasures your contact,
Every single word,
Only in His time
Will the answer be heard.

Known only to "Thee"
Your quiet whispers come to light,
He wants to know your everything,
You are precious in His sight.

In the realms of Heaven,
A life time away,
Your quiet whispers are stored
In His light that will never fade.

A love so deep and pure
Can only be from God,
Your quiet whispers are received
At His Throne of Gold.

JOYS OF HEAVEN

The joys of heaven are felt
Within the human heart,
Moments of such splendour
Will leave their mark.

Divine intervention
From the Holy Spirit Himself,
Bringing the joy of heaven,
Is truly felt.

Earth's cares recede
Into the back-drops of the mind,
The joy of heaven reflects
Into this heart of mine.

Such peace I know,
The joy of heaven so real,
Of Jesus Christ the Redeemer
Is what I surely feel.

Pure sweetness waits ahead,
The joys of heaven can be yours,
His power and glory will meet you,
He'll be waiting at heaven's door!

LIFE SAVING BALM

Lord, Your Holy Spirit sweetly comes
With His life saving balm,
His beauty ever pure
As I seek His loving arms.

In His saving balm
I know His love so real,
He brings God's grace and mercy,
My wounds and scars He heals.

I surrender them to Him,
In trust and faith I come,
To His place of worship
Where I receive His saving balm.

Through God's forgiving love
I receive life saving balm,
It comes from His Spirit
Who brings His peace and calm.

QUALIFIED IN YOUR LOVE

I'm qualified in Your love Lord
When I give my heart to You,
It will take many years of lessons
To qualify it's true.

In Your love I have security
And reassurance all my life,
That You are my Redeemer,
Who paid a great sacrifice.

I'm qualified in Your love Lord
To know the right from wrong,
I pray for Your guidance
For me to lean upon.

I'm qualified in Your love Lord,
A sinner who saw Your light,
Keep me focused on the high road
And forever in Your sight.

I'm qualified in Your love Lord,
I can expect to receive,
A blessing of the Holy Spirit
So I can sow eternal seeds.

PART FOUR

"…I was born and came into the world for this one
purpose, to speak about the truth…"

John 18 : 37

JESUS SHOWED GREAT MERCY…
HE TOOK OUR SIN TO THE CROSS…

"Jesus said, "Forgive them, Father!
They don't know what they are doing."

Luke 23 : 34

KING OF MERCY

There is a King of Mercy
His reign will never end,
He came to earth to show us
How to live and to repent.

Without His Holy teaching
We could never understand,
Why we should try to forgive
The hurts from our fellow man.

Even from the Cross He cried,
"Forgive them Father! They don't know what they are doing."
The King of Mercy still loved you
In His time of suffering.

He cared so much for mankind,
He paid a debt we could never afford,
Because He is the King of Mercy
He cancelled the sin for one and all.

His Name is Jesus
And He loves you from Eternity,
Whatever wrong you have done in this life
A pardon you will receive.

His angels will roar for you
When you carry mercy on your path,
A blessing beyond compare,
Now the King of Mercy lives in your heart.

GOOD ENOUGH FOR A PARDON

Are we good enough for a pardon Lord?
Our shame brings its doubts,
But You are love itself Lord
That's what Calvary was about!

Are we good enough for a pardon Lord?
Our guilt surely says "no"
But by the will of the Heavenly Father
A young Nazarene thought so!

He took our sin to Calvary,
It was His Father's call,
He was nailed to a wooden Cross,
He took the sin of all.

The Son of God came to earth
For that one day at Calvary,
So we can have eternal life
And a pardon to receive!

For a pardon for every sin
We only have to believe,
He took the Cross for us
And He rose to victory!

LOOK INTO THE EYES OF THE SAVIOUR

Look into the eyes of the Saviour
Who came to save the world,
He carried our sin to a Cross
But His gaze on Heaven He held.

No lie He ever told,
No sin was ever found,
He was born humbly in a stable,
Almighty God; the Son of Man.

He prayed in the garden
This sacrifice would pass Him by,
But He obeyed His Father's will,
He would live, but first, He would die!

Prophecy revealed the Lamb of God
Would come as a Sacrifice,
A debt we can never pay,
We can only look into His eyes.

He came with the gift of salvation
So we can have eternal life,
He paid for the sin of man,
We can only look into His eyes.

He looked beyond the grave
To His Throne in Paradise,
Where He would dwell forever
With His Father by His side.

ANGELS ROAR…
CHRIST IS ALIVE…

"Let us give thanks to the God and Father of our
Lord Jesus Christ! Because of his great mercy he gave
us new life by raising Jesus Christ from death.
This fills us with a living hope…"

1 Peter 1 : 3

THE SPLENDOUR IN THE GARDEN

There's splendour in the garden,
Wonder and awe all around,
The Saviour risen from the grave,
Great joy, great joy is found.

His magnificence in the garden
Overcomes morning song,
The sweetest lingering fragrance,
To the world now belongs.

Majesty all around,
His light outshines the world,
There's splendour in the garden,
Now, all is well!

The Cross stands empty
And the grave is open wide,
There's splendour in the garden,
Christ now lives for you and I.

CROWN OF LIFE

There's eternal life forever,
The Saviour raised from the grave,
A Crown of Life He wears,
His life for you He gave.

His Heavenly Father gave Him victory,
No more darkness to bear,
The grave now wide open,
A Crown of Life He wears.

He strolled through the garden,
His transfiguration taken place,
Glorified in heavenly splendour,
Wounds from the Cross erased.

In awe and in wonder
The precious Saviour lives,
A Crown of Life He wears,
Eternal Life He gives.

Beyond our understanding,
He gave His life for all,
Living, victorious King of Kings,
"I believe" is the call!

THE HOLY CHRIST CAME QUIETLY…
THE SAVIOUR OF THE WORLD…

"There were some shepherds in that part of the country
who were spending the night in the fields, taking care of their
flocks. An angel of the Lord appeared to them, and the
glory of the Lord shone over them…."Don't be afraid! I
am here with good news for you, which will bring great joy
to all people. This very day in David's town your
Saviour was born – Christ the Lord!..."

Luke 2 : 8 - 11

THE HUMBLE STABLE

Angels proclaimed His birth
To the shepherds in the fields,
Singing with great joy,
Messiah's birth revealed.

In the humble stable at Bethlehem
The Messiah King made His way,
Laid gently in the Manger
In swaddling clothes He lay.

The Holiest of nights
In the winter deep,
Mary cuddled her baby,
Her new-born Messiah King.

In awe and wonder
They worshipped the new-born King,
The Wisemen saw His Star
Shining bright in the East.

What joy was proclaimed
On that Holy night,
Humbly in the stable
The new born Holy Christ.

YOU ARE THE PERFECT GIFT LORD

Precious Lord You came to earth
On the Holiest of nights,
In the stable You were born,
The Star of the East shone bright.

On this Holy night
Salvation You became,
Mankind You adored,
Our lives forever changed.

You are the perfect gift Lord
In every possible way,
Nothing can compare
Saviour of the world You became.

Your mission was clear,
No doubt in Your mind,
You would pay for our transgressions
To allow eternal life.

We can only open our hearts
So You can live within,
Through the precious Holy Spirit,
Our heart change can begin.

GOODWILL IN THE AIR

Christmas time so special,
There's goodwill in the air,
Christmas time rejoice,
The Saviour is here!

There's goodwill in the air,
The gift of love is known,
Brought by the Messiah,
Our heart He wants to own.

There is a sense of giving,
Just as the Magi did before,
Holy gifts for the new-born King
Who they came to adore.

We can lay aside misgivings
To replace with love and care,
The Saviour came to show us
That He is always there.

Christ is born tonight,
From Heaven's Throne He came,
Heavenly angels roar,
Blessed He will remain.

GLORIOUS PRINCE OF PEACE

The Saviour of the world,
Born that Holy night,
Came to live amongst us,
He would be our Shining Light.

Our glorious Prince of Peace,
No sin in Him to find,
His message of love and peace
Was for all mankind.

His eternal mercy and grace
He renews every day,
Our glorious Prince of Peace
Will always remain.

The Magi came to worship Him
With gifts from afar,
Frankincense, Myrrh and Gold,
They were led by the Eastern Star.

What wonder and glory shone that night
And filled the stable stall,
Shepherds came to worship
They were filled with awe.

Our glorious Prince of Peace,
Lord of Lords and King of Kings,
Forever and ever our Saviour,
His reign will never end.

ALSO BY CLAIRE GROSE

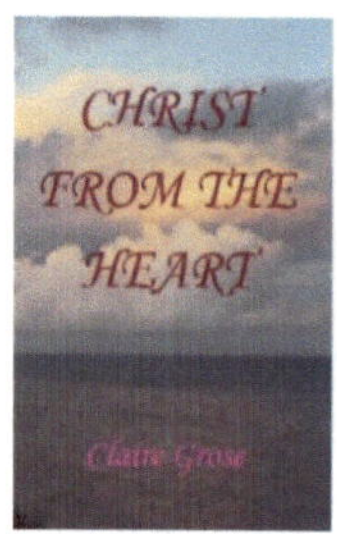

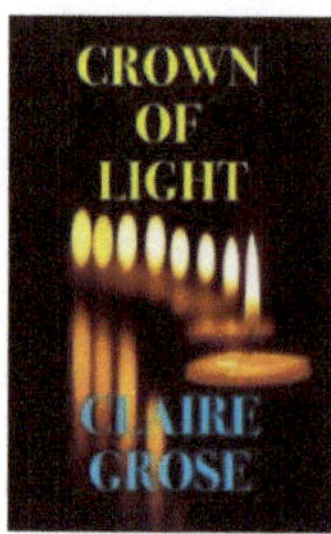

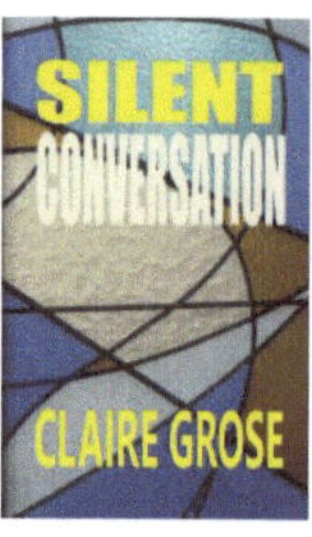

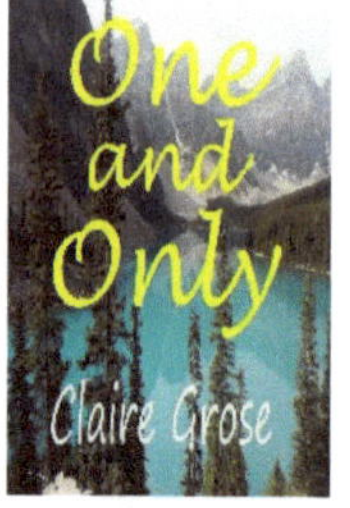

ABOUT THE AUTHOR

Claire worked as a Government Public Servant in the Lands Department, Adelaide, South Australia until she married and became a mother of two boys.

She later returned to the work force during which time she gained a "Living Hope" Phone Counselling certificate which influenced her need to help others.

Through this and personal experience she found herself inspired by God's love to put pen to paper.

PHOTO CREDITS

COVER PHOTO: Veale Gardens, Adelaide taken by Claire Grose

Page 2: Bird Bath; S.A. – Claire Grose
Page 12: Cattle and Autumn Trees; Qld - Claire Grose
Page 24: Eboney; S.A. – Claire Grose
Page 31: Frangipani Tree; Qld – Carol Turner
Page 39: Windchimes; Qld – Claire Grose
Page 47: Chain of Hearts plant; Qld. – Carol Turner
Page 55: Nandina plants S.A. – Michael & Andrea
Page 70: Wattle Tree; S.A. – Michael & Andrea
Page 78: Mixed Flower Bouquet; S.A. – Claire Grose
Page 87: Salisbury Uniting Church; S.A. – Claire Grose
Page 92: Salisbury Uniting Church; S.A. – Claire Grose
Page 96: Lavender Garden; S.A. – Lynne Phillips